Midnight Teddies

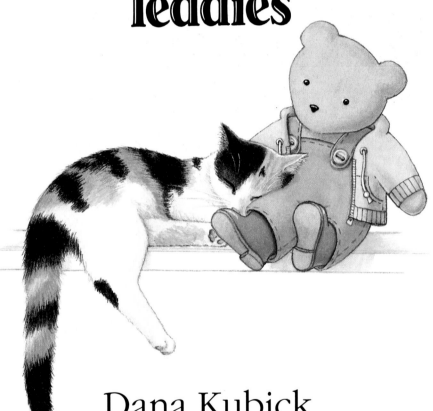

Dana Kubick

DISCOVERY TOYS, INC.

Teddy had been Jessica's special bear for as long as he could remember. Of course, that wasn't so very long, because Teddy was a very young bear. Wherever Jessica went, Teddy went too – and Jessica's favorite place was the attic.

In the attic, she read books or played with toys and puzzles. But today Jessica had the key to the big old trunk, which she had never opened. In it she found hats as big as frying-pans and silky gowns that had come all the way from China.

Jessica loved dress-up games and she always dressed up Teddy too. He liked that!

What Teddy didn't like was to be left alone in the attic. In fact, it had never ever happened before. But this evening, when it was time for bed, Jessica simply forgot Teddy. And although he was an extremely clever bear, Teddy could not wriggle nor twitch nor move a single muscle – at least not until midnight, the hour when toys can come to life. To make matters worse, a book was poking him rather uncomfortably in the back.
Even more annoying,
the trunk began to talk.
Teddy distinctly
heard it say, "Help!"

It seemed a long time before the downstairs clock struck twelve. Then Teddy felt himself shiver and quiver. He managed to move the uncomfortable book just a little. He wiggled his toes, then he shook his legs, and suddenly he leapt to his feet.

"Help!" cried the voice again.

Teddy had never heard of a talking trunk, and his fur stood on end. Then he realized that it was not the trunk crying for help, but someone inside it!

"Who's there?" he whispered, peering over the edge.

To Teddy's surprise, out climbed two bears. But what strange, dusty bears they were!

"I'm Theodore," said the one in the sailor suit.

"I'm Ned," said the one in the old-fashioned cardigan. Ned was badly in need of repair. He was coming unstitched in several places.

"We're so glad to see you. We were put away years and years ago, when our children grew up. It's been terribly boring closed in the trunk with no one to play with."

"Theodore is horrid," complained Ned. "When he can't think of anything else to do, he tickles."

"Well," said Teddy. "Tonight we can play together."

Because he was the bear of the house, Teddy led the way. Theodore and Ned followed him to the top of the stairs, then they all went down – bumpety-bump, bumpety-bump – one step after another, until all three landed in a heap at the bottom.

Clouds of dust flew up around the two old bears, especially Theodore, who sneezed. "Atishoo! Atishoo!"

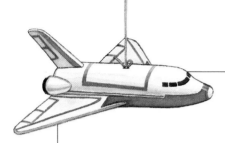

Teddy was alarmed. What if someone had heard the thumps and bumps and sneezes? He tiptoed to Jessica's bedroom and opened the door. Silly Lilly opened one eye, but otherwise no one stirred. He opened the next door

"Who's that?" asked Ned.

"Jessica's brother," said Teddy. "But he doesn't like bears. He likes jets and rockets."

"What's a jet?" said Theodore.

"What's a rocket?" said Ned.

Teddy stared at them. What a long time they had been in the trunk if they didn't know about jets and rockets!

But the two old bears were even more puzzled when Teddy suggested they play in the bathroom. Theodore and Ned had never seen such gleaming faucets or so many complicated handles. Theodore tried them all.

Suddenly, water showered down from above his head! Poor Ned was soaked. He had wanted to play with the plastic ducks and fish and boats – plastic was something very different indeed!

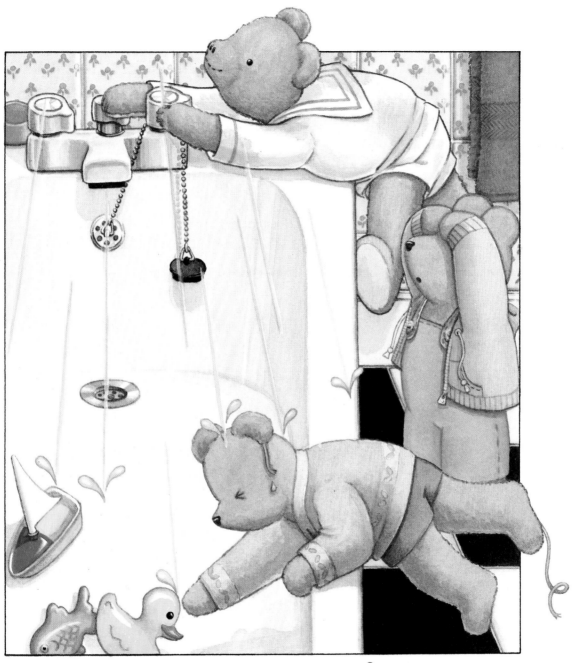

Next, Teddy took his two new friends downstairs. In the kitchen, there were even more knobs and switches and handles. Theodore actually felt quite giddy with excitement.

Teddy opened the refrigerator and a light came on.

"It's magic!" said Theodore.

"No," said Teddy. "It's electricity."

Theodore shut the refrigerator door, then opened it, shut it and opened it, just to see the light go off and on. He stood on his tip-toe but he couldn't reach the magic light. So he stood on his tallest tip-toes, grabbed the shelf and pulled himself up.

Whoosh! Down came the tub of yogurt.

Zoom! went Teddy . . . and caught it just in time.

Teddy, being used to electric lights, was more interested in the food. Yogurt was his favorite and he took a little taste (or two, or three) before he put the pot back on the shelf. He didn't notice Theodore clinging to the refrigerator door. And certainly no one saw the pot of strawberry jam – until, that is, it was suddenly all over the floor!

Teddy was horrified. "Quickly!" he gasped. "Get a cloth! Get a mop!"

The three bears wiped and mopped until there wasn't a bit of strawberry jam left on the floor. By then, Teddy had decided that the kitchen was rather a frightening place.

But the living room wasn't any safer, for Theodore found switches irresistible. Without warning, he turned on the television and filled the room with noise.

"Turn it off!" Teddy shouted.

But poor Theodore and Ned simply stared at the television in amazement.

Teddy flicked off the switch himself, but not quickly enough. Lights went on upstairs; voices called. The bears hid. They heard footsteps in the hall. The door opened and someone big peered in and then went away again.

"Let's go back upstairs," Teddy said, and the others agreed. They had had enough excitement for one evening.

The next day, as soon as it was light, Jessica realized that Teddy was missing and she ran to the attic. "Poor Teddy!" she said. "I forgot you."

Of course Teddy couldn't say a word or twitch a muscle.

Then Jessica noticed some fur peeking from under her dress-up clothes. "Who are you?" she asked, pulling out the two old bears.

And then she discovered something else – an album of photographs tucked into the lining of the trunk. Turning the pages, she saw pictures of Theodore, all clean and new and there was Ned, in another photograph, on a picnic.

"You're family bears!" Jessica exclaimed and, picking them up, she took all three to her room.

There, Jessica brushed and sponged the old bears. She put a button on Theodore's trousers and gave Ned new stitches where he was coming undone. She put their photographs on her wall and added one of herself with Teddy.

Then she sat the bears together on her bed. Already they looked the best of friends.

And so they were. The only thing that puzzled Jessica was that all three bears smelled faintly of strawberry jam.

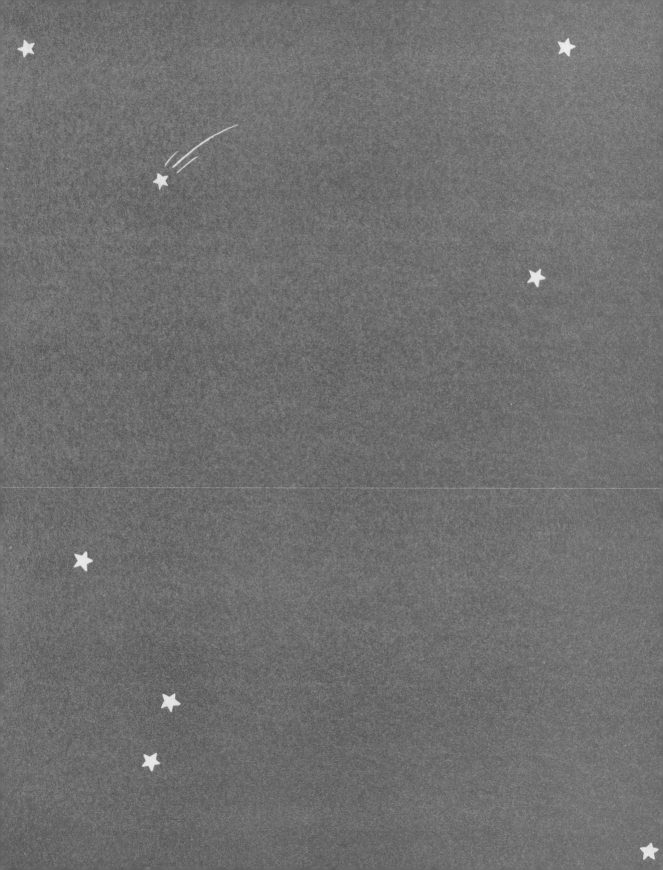